Once there was a boy who was very
very
very little.

He was smaller
than a cornstalk.

He was smaller than a baseball bat.

He was smaller than his sled.

He was smaller than his father's workbench.

And smaller than a broom.

He was too little to be in the parade passing by.

He couldn't feed the pony at the petting zoo.

He couldn't touch the
pedals on his bicycle

or reach the cookie jar in the kitchen.

He had to have a special little chair to sit on and a special little table to eat at

and a special little bed to sleep in.

He was smaller than all the
other little boys on his street.

BUT

One day he could reach
the pedals on his bicycle.

He could push the
supermarket cart.

He was bigger than his dog!
And bigger than his sled!

Every day after that he found more things which were smaller than he.

The very little boy began to grow BIGGER!

He grew as big as a cornstalk in the spring.

He grew BIGGER
than a baseball bat.

He could even push
the broom by himself.

He was big enough to be in the parade.

He could feed the pony at the petting zoo.

He could see the top of his
father's workbench

and get a cookie all by himself.

He grew too BIG for his special little
chair and his special little table
and his special little bed.

Now he ate at the big table with
his mother and father

and he had a new big bed.

He was no longer a very little boy.

He was big enough to play with
the other little boys on his street.

Now he was big enough to be a big
brother to his brand-new baby sister

who was very
  very
    very little!